The CRIMSON COMET

story and pictures by DEAN MORRISSEY
written by DEAN MORRISSEY
and STEPHEN KRENSKY

HARPERCOLLINS Publishers

for KELLY, TERENCE, and IAN

—D.M.

Count the stars up in the sky.
The Man-in-the-Moon is flying by,
Shining through darkness all around.
Sleepy heads nod, safe and sound.

If only that were true, thought Nora.
But she was wide awake.
She looked up at the twinkling stars,
and the moon, once so bright,
suddenly blinked out.

"J-a-a-a-c-k!" she cried, scurrying down the hall.
"The moon, the moon. It's gone!"
"Okay, okay," said her brother. "Calm down!"
He took a look for himself.
"You're right. We'd better check this out."
"But how?" Nora asked.
Jack pointed to his rocket.
"We're going in *that*!" said Nora.
"*That*," said Jack, "is the Crimson Comet."

Nora and Jack climbed into the cockpit.
"Hurry up!" said Nora. "This is an emergency."
But Jack checked his instruments carefully.
He didn't want to end up on Mars by mistake.

Very soon the rocket blasted out the bedroom window and into the night. Nora looked around her and plucked a few stars from the sky.

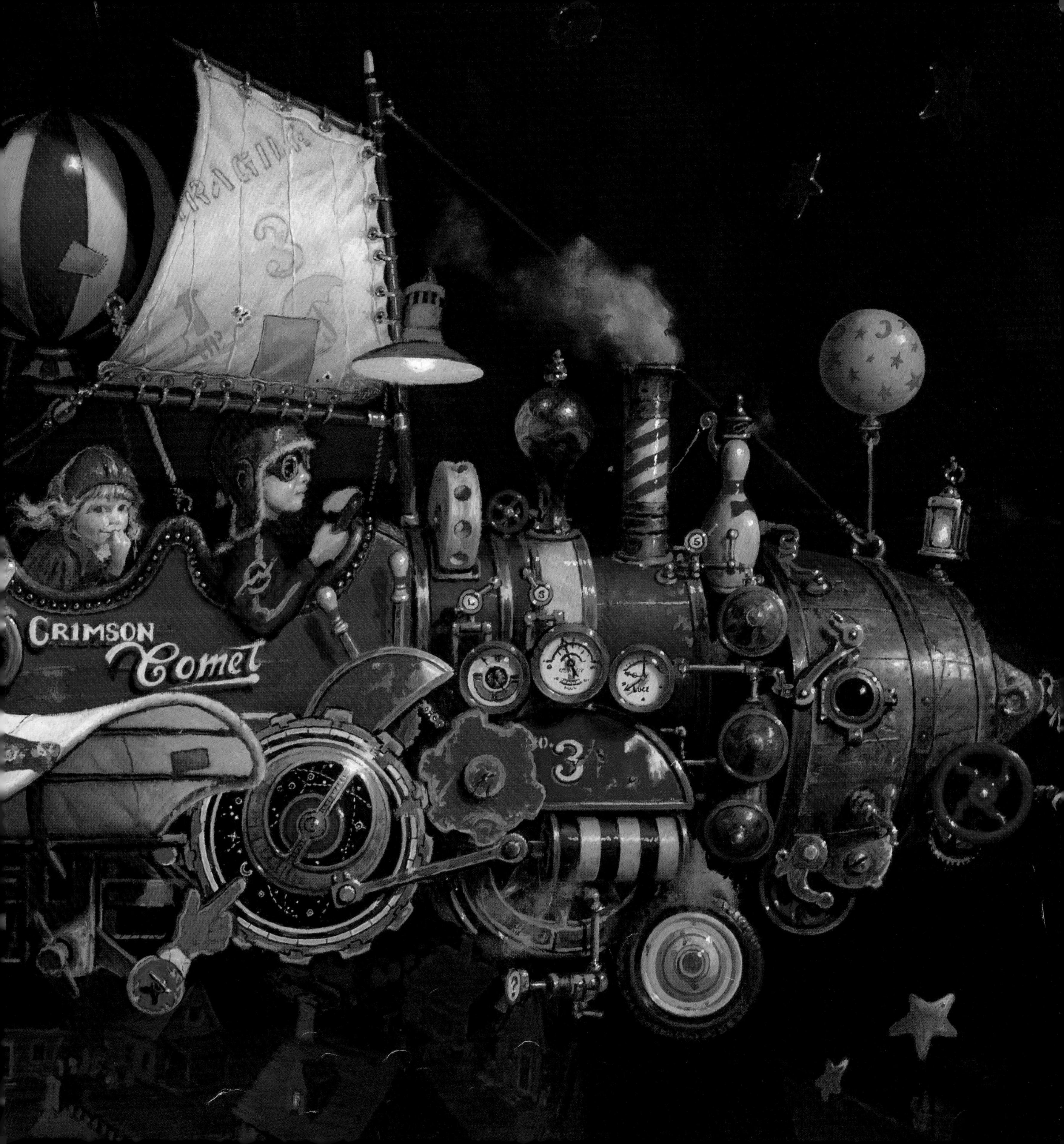
CRIMSON
Comet
3

Up and up and up they went until . . .
THUNK!
The rocket stopped cold.
"Uh-oh," said Nora.
They got out for a better look.
"I think we hit the—" Jack began.

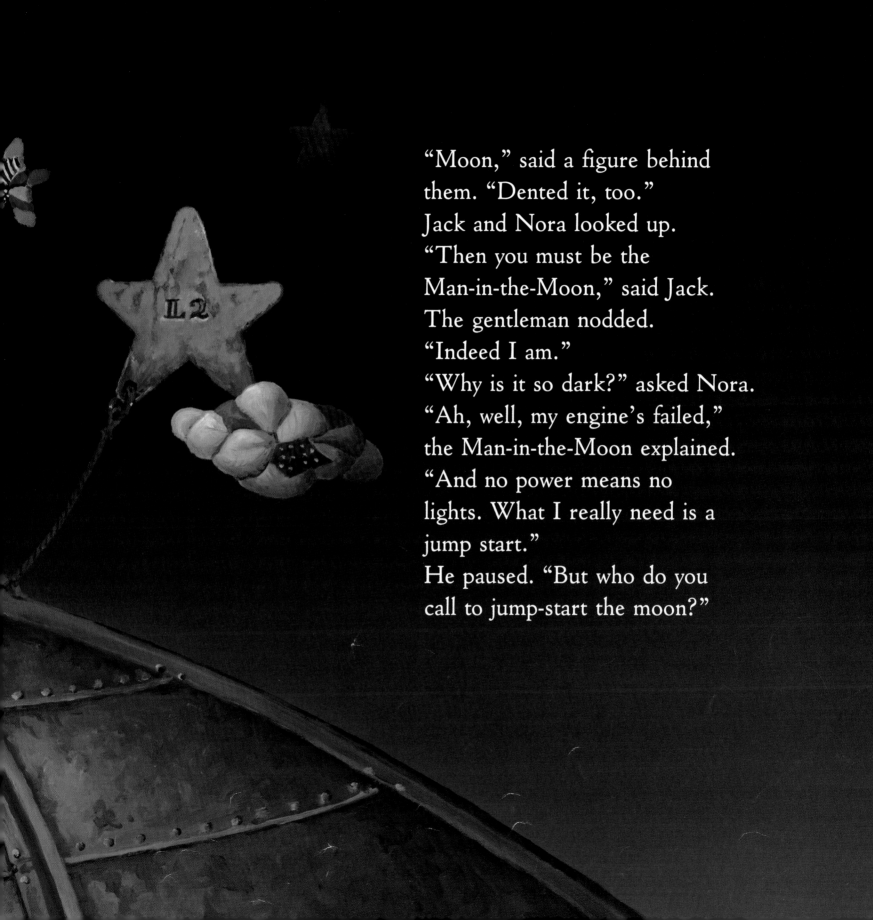

"Moon," said a figure behind them. "Dented it, too."
Jack and Nora looked up.
"Then you must be the Man-in-the-Moon," said Jack.
The gentleman nodded. "Indeed I am."
"Why is it so dark?" asked Nora.
"Ah, well, my engine's failed," the Man-in-the-Moon explained. "And no power means no lights. What I really need is a jump start."
He paused. "But who do you call to jump-start the moon?"

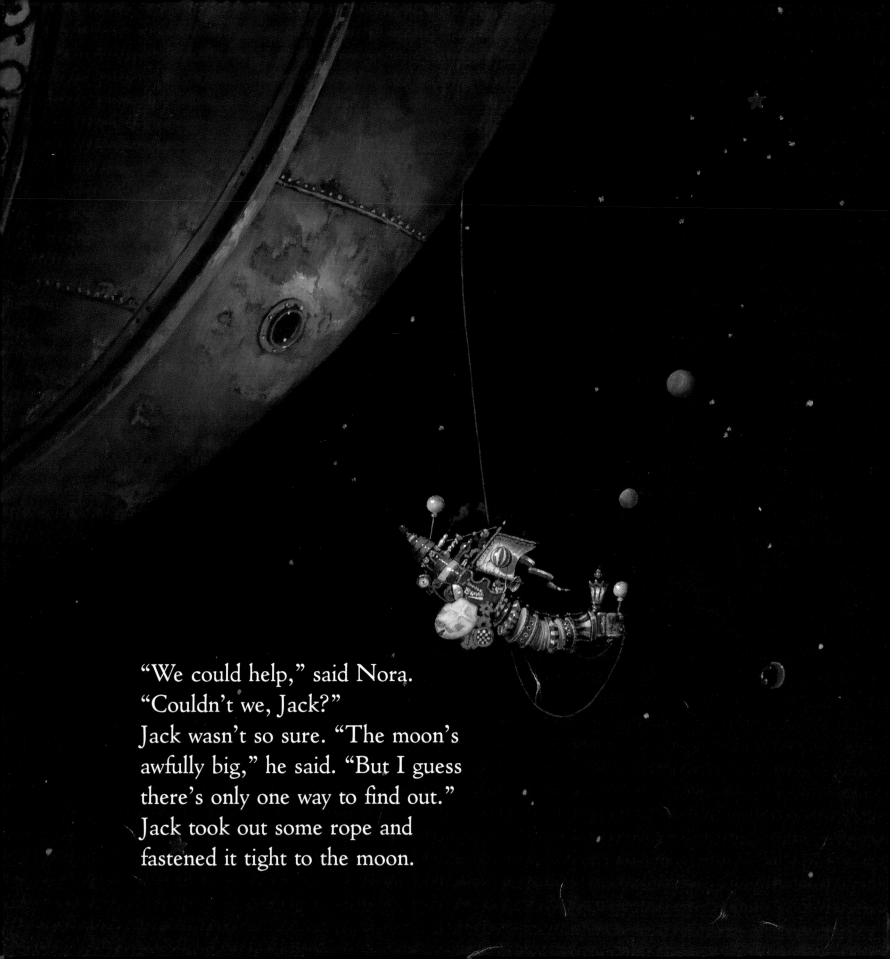

"We could help," said Nora.
"Couldn't we, Jack?"
Jack wasn't so sure. "The moon's
awfully big," he said. "But I guess
there's only one way to find out."
Jack took out some rope and
fastened it tight to the moon.

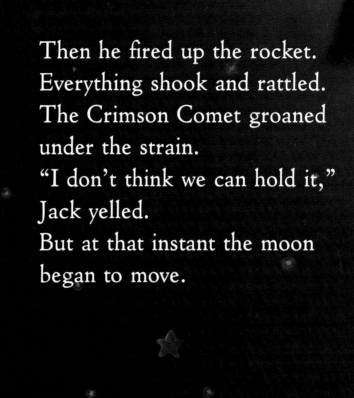

Then he fired up the rocket.
Everything shook and rattled.
The Crimson Comet groaned
under the strain.
"I don't think we can hold it,"
Jack yelled.
But at that instant the moon
began to move.

PUTT-PHLUTTER-PLUTTT . . . .

The moon's engine rumbled to life.
Its lanterns began to glow.
"Hooray!" cried Nora.
"The Crimson Comet saves the day,"
said Jack, retrieving his rope.
The Man-in-the-Moon waved in thanks
as the moon drifted away.

Jack checked his instruments again
and set a course for home.
But the fuel gauge read empty!

Down, down, down they went.
Faster and faster.
"We need something to burn!" Jack shouted.
Then Nora remembered the stars.
She threw them in the firebox, and the
engine flared to life, slowing the ship's fall.

BAMMMM!

The Crimson Comet bumped

and bashed

and crumpled

and . . . *CRASHED.*

Jack looked up from the broken rocket.
"We made it!" he said. "Are you all right?"
"I think so," said Nora.
She climbed out of her seat.
"And there's the moon. Right where it should be."
They both smiled at it.

And

just

for

a

moment,

they

thought

the

moon

smiled

back.

The Crimson Comet   Copyright © 2006 by Dean Morrissey   Story and pictures by Dean Morrissey   Written by Dean Morrissey and Stephen Krensky   Manufactured in China.   All rights reserved. No part of this book may be used or reproduced in any manner whatsoever without written permission except in the case of brief quotations embodied in critical articles and reviews. For information address HarperCollins Children's Books, a division of HarperCollins Publishers, 1350 Avenue of the Americas, New York, NY 10019.   www.harperchildrens.com

Library of Congress Cataloging-in-Publication Data   Morrissey, Dean.   The crimson comet / story and pictures by Dean Morrissey ; written by Dean Morrissey and Stephen Krensky.—1st ed.   p.   cm.   Summary: When the light on the moon goes out, Nora and her brother Jack take a trip in their rocket to help the Man-in-the-Moon regain power.   ISBN-10: 0-06-008068-X (trade bdg.) — ISBN-13: 978-0-06-008068-6 (trade bdg.)   ISBN-10: 0-06-008070-1 (lib. bdg.) — ISBN-13: 978-0-06-008070-9 (lib. bdg.)   [1. Moon—Fiction. 2. Bedtime—Fiction. 3. Rockets (Aeronautics)—Fiction. 4. Brothers and sisters—Fiction.] I. Krensky, Stephen. II. Title.   PZ7.M84532Cr 2006   2004025978   [E]—dc22   Design by Stephanie Bart-Horvath
1 2 3 4 5 6 7 8 9 10   ❖   First Edition